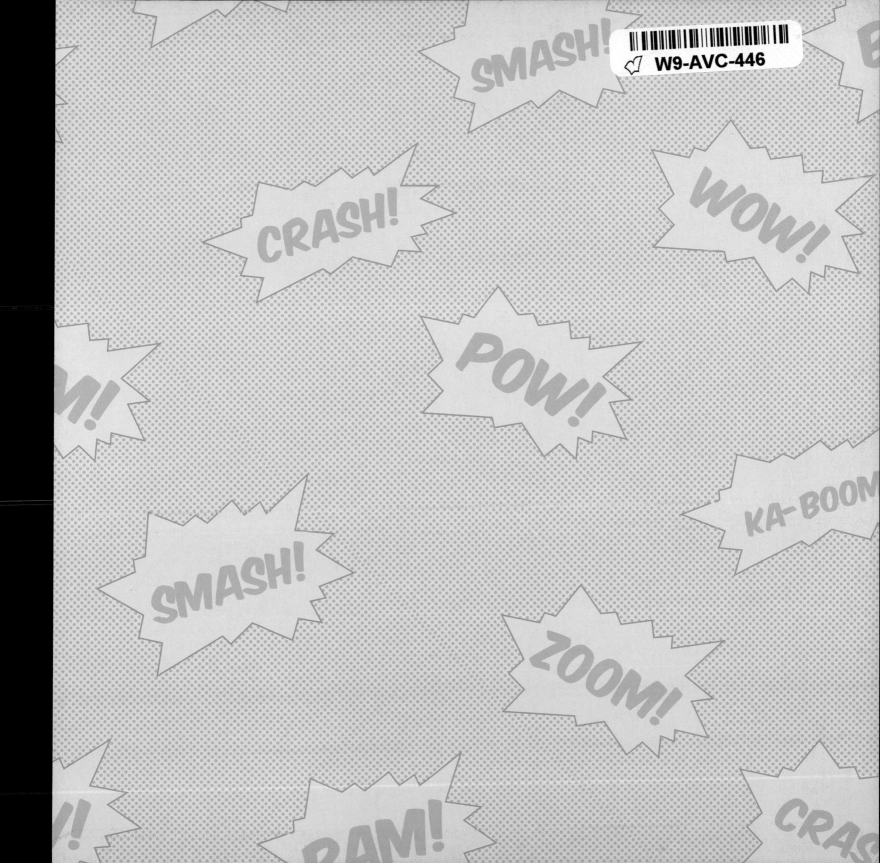

Written by Brooke Dworkin. Illustrated by Val Semeiks and Hi-Fi Design. Based on the Marvel comic book series *Hulk* and *X-Men*.

Printed in China
First Edition
1 3 5 7 9 10 8 6 4 2
978-1-4847-0415-8
T425-2382-5-13338

marvelkids.com

Published by Marvel Press, an imprint of Disney Book Group. No part of this book may be reproduced or transmitted in any form or by any means, electronic or mechanical, including photocopying, recording, or by any information storage and retrieval system, without written permission from the publisher. For information address Marvel Press, 1101 Flower Street, Glendale, California 91201.

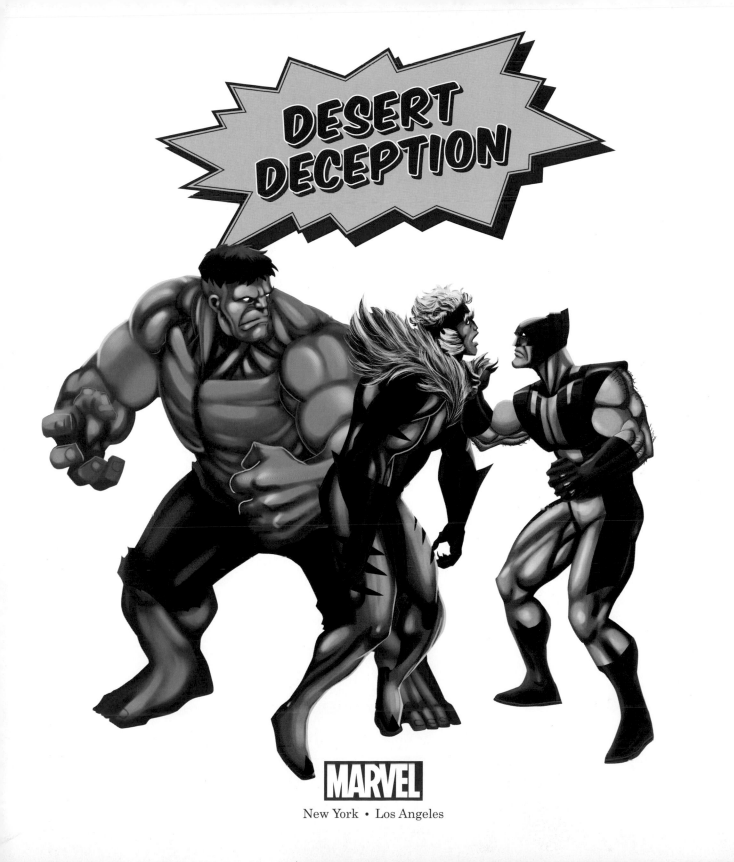

MARVEL

New York • Los Angeles

Bruce Banner was on a mission to find a mutant—or, rather, two mutants. He had heard that Wolverine was battling another mutant nearby and was curious to study the two. Maybe he could learn something that would help him control Hulk.

Bruce also knew that if things didn't go well for Wolverine, he might need Hulk's help. But there was one thing Bruce wasn't counting on . . . the army!

General "Thunderbolt" Ross had been trying to catch Bruce since the first time he turned into Hulk. Knowing that Bruce was fascinated by mutants, the general had spread a rumor about Wolverine's fight. He was sure it would lure Bruce to the secret army base, and he was right.

Bruce was angry with himself for getting caught. How could he be so stupid as to walk right into a trap?

Bruce's anger grew and grew until he could not control it anymore.

But General Ross was ready for Hulk. Firing an experimental gamma ray at the green giant, he temporarily weakened Hulk enough to lock him up.

The next morning, over at the Xavier mansion, Wolverine received some strange news: he was rumored to be fighting another mutant in the desert.

Wolverine knew a trick when he heard one, and he was sure he knew just who was being tricked. Wolverine's friend Hulk lived in the desert. If someone was spreading rumors about Wolverine's being out there, that person might be trying to trap Hulk. And so, jumping on his motorcycle, Wolverine raced into the desert to see if Hulk needed his help.

It didn't take Wolverine long to find traces of Hulk. He was being held at a secret army base!

Wolverine broke into the compound. Inside, he found the gamma-ray machine. Realizing it must have been used against his friend, Wolverine quickly destroyed the weapon.

Wolverine found Hulk, and the two broke out of the compound together.

Free of the compound, the two friends set out for
Hulk's home.

They had not gone far when Wolverine heard a loud
snarl. He turned around to see the villainous
Sabretooth lunging at him. The mutant
had been searching for Wolverine!

Sabretooth knocked Wolverine down and then, growling, jumped onto a ledge above Hulk's head.

But Hulk was faster—and stronger—than Sabretooth expected. Scooping up a huge boulder, Hulk heaved it at the mutant. The giant rock shattered into a million tiny pebbles.

Sabretooth scurried
away from the boulder
just in time, but again,
Hulk was faster. Snatching
up the mutant, he hurled
him against the cave wall.

As Sabretooth stumbled to his feet, Wolverine flew at him, kicking him back into the wall.

Wolverine looked down at his fallen rival. Sabretooth
groaned. Then, suddenly, his eyes grew large.

Turning around, Wolverine saw Hulk holding a giant boulder. He was about to throw it at Sabretooth.

"Wait!" Wolverine called. "He's had enough!"

Wolverine grabbed the defeated villain and pulled him close.

"I could finish you off, but I won't. That's the difference between you and me, Sabretooth. You're an animal. But I'm better than that. And besides, I have other plans for you. . . ."

Turning to Hulk, Wolverine said, "Thanks for the help. I couldn't have stopped him without you."

Patting Wolverine on the back, Hulk smiled and nodded.

A short while later, Wolverine climbed back on his bike and waved good-bye to Hulk. Inside the cave, Sabretooth lay tied up in a corner. Hulk would be leaving him for the army to find.

After all, General Ross *had* been looking for a beast. . . .